I Don't Draw, I COLOR!

Adam Lehrhaupt

illustrated by Felicita Sala

A Paula Wiseman Book

Simon & Schuster Books for Young Readers

NEW YORK   LONDON   TORONTO   SYDNEY   NEW DELHI

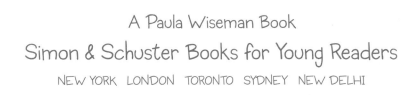

Some people are really good at drawing.

But *my* puppies look like **mush.**

My cars look like **lumps.** . . . .

Or like **boxes** . . .

Or this.

Do these look like people to you?

I didn't think so.

So, I don't draw.

I color.

When I color, I can express myself
without *drawing* anything.

By using different hues . . .

Red.

Blue.

Yellow.

And by changing my lines . . .

Thick.

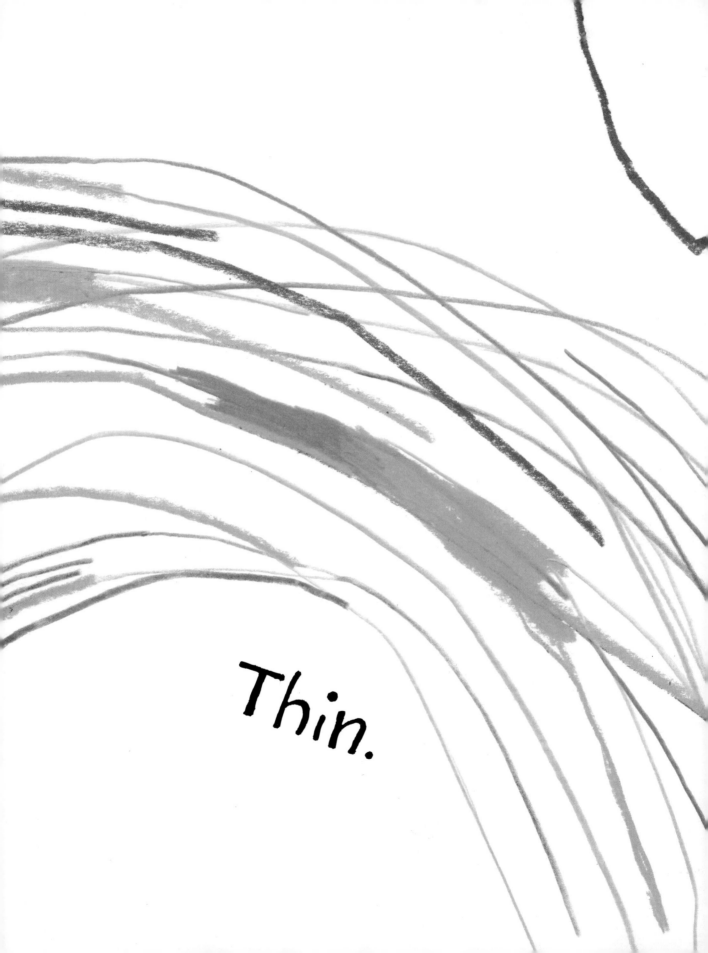

Thin.

squiggly.

Jagged.

I can show . . .

Happy.

Calm.

I can even show

scary.

Or something full of

life.

So when someone asks,
"Do you want to draw?"

I say, "No, thanks.
I don't draw.

I color."

And I can color
anything.

Can't I. . . .

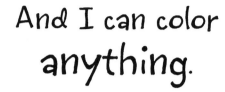

What makes you
YOU?

Create a
self-portrait

Am I a dark and sad
blue?

Or a bright, happy
yellow?

A messy, dark
brown?

Or an excited
orange?

I am *more* than just
one of these things.

Sometimes I'm happy.

Other times I'm sad.

I've even been messy.

Excited.

And scared.

I'm a whole

jumble

of things.

All tumbled together.

A colorful masterpiece.

What colors are you?

For the many teachers who supported my creativity,
no matter what form it took
—A. L.

For Emanuela, who stopped drawing a long time ago,
but who made my childhood so very colorful
—F. S.

SIMON & SCHUSTER BOOKS FOR YOUNG READERS
An imprint of Simon & Schuster Children's Publishing Division
1230 Avenue of the Americas, New York, New York 10020
Text copyright © 2017 by Adam Lehrhaupt
Illustrations copyright © 2017 by Felicita Sala
SIMON & SCHUSTER BOOKS FOR YOUNG READERS is a trademark of Simon & Schuster, Inc.
For information about special discounts for bulk purchases, please contact
Simon & Schuster Special Sales at 1-866-506-1949 or business@simonandschuster.com.
The Simon & Schuster Speakers Bureau can bring authors to your live event. For more information or to book an event,
contact the Simon & Schuster Speakers Bureau at 1-866-248-3049 or visit our website at www.simonspeakers.com.
Book design by Laurent Linn
The text for this book was set in Joppa.
The illustrations for this book were rendered in watercolors, drawing and colored pencils, and crayons.
Manufactured in China
1216 SCP
First Edition
2 4 6 8 10 9 7 5 3 1
Library of Congress Cataloging-in-Publication Data
Names: Lehrhaupt, Adam, author. | Sala, Felicita, illustrator.
Title: I don't draw, I color! / Adam Lehrhaupt ; illustrated by Felicita Sala.
Other titles: I do not draw, I color!
Description: First Edition. | New York : Simon & Schuster Books for Young Readers, [2017] | "A Paula Wiseman Book." | Summary: "A boy discovers that
even if he does not draw, he can be an artist and express himself through coloring"—Provided by publisher.
Identifiers: LCCN 2016010819 |
ISBN 9781481462754 (hardback) | ISBN 9781481462761 (eBook)
Subjects: | CYAC: Drawing—Fiction. | Colors—Fiction. | Imagination—Fiction. | BISAC: JUVENILE FICTION / Art & Architecture. | JUVENILE
FICTION / Concepts / Colors. | JUVENILE FICTION / Imagination & Play.
Classification: LCC PZ7.L532745 Iam 2017 | DDC [E]—dc23
LC record available at https://lccn.loc.gov/2016010819